breathe

healing conversations

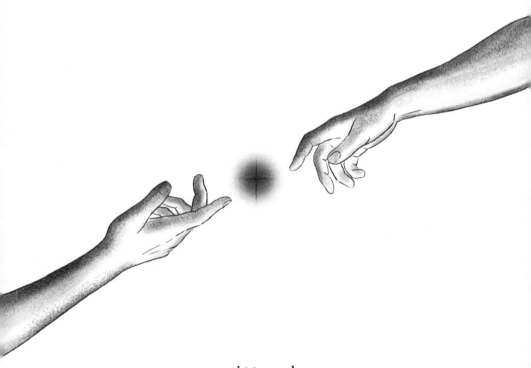

written by

Karen Achille

Breathe: Healing Conversations
Published by Karen Achille

ACHILLE, KAREN
BREATHE: HEALING CONVERSATIONS
KAREN ACHILLE

ISBN : 979-8-9856974-0-7

The book is printed in United States.

Dedication

To my twin flames, for encouraging me to grow even when it seemed impossible.

Mom, for teaching me that love is truly unconditional. Alex, for teaching me that self-love is necessary and empowering. Jay, for teaching me that chivalry is still alive. Mika, although you've transitioned, our 34 years of sisterhood has taught me that love can be expressed in many ways. Last, but not least, Gayle, my muse, for simply being the purest manifestation of intimate love. Without you, none of this would be possible.

Table of Contents

Dedication iii

PURGING

Insufficient Funds 1

Unfortunate Truth 2

Self-Reflection 3

Candid Truth 4

Self-Worth 5

Damaged Goods 6

Drained 7

Self-Reflection 8

Broken 9

Hide 11

Parasite 12

Confused 13

BREATHE

Memories 14

Hide & Seek 16

Awakening 17

If It Sounds Like You, It's You 20

Blurred Lines 21

Selfish 22

Forgiveness 23

ASKING

Manifestation 25

Necessary Lessons 26

Complacent 27

Broken Spirit 28

Victim to Victor 29

Truth 30

Self-Destruction 31

Guilty 32

Intuition 33

Choices 34

Hard Truth 35

SHIFTING

Tough Conversations 37

Vulnerability 38

Soul Work 39

Self-Hypnosis 40

Preparation 41

Normalize Self-Love 42

The Rage We Carry 43

ALLOWING

Expectations 45

In Love with Me 46

Ode to My Single Mother 47

Acknowledging Mom 48

Own Your Shit 49

Clarity 50

Choose Wisely 51

Energy 52

Time 53

SURRENDERING

Beautiful Dilemma 55

Exposed 56

Falling 57

Mental Orgasm 58

Surrendering in Love 59

Easy to Love 60

Long Distance Relationship Struggles 61

Frustrated 62

Little Things 63

Overthinking 64

Lovers then Friends 65

Space 66

Blinded 67

Soul Resonance 68

Thoughts become Things 69

RECEIVING

Invested 71

Walking Blindly in Love 72

Unconditional Prayer 73

CPR 74

Soul Love 75

Contrast 76

Post-Relationship Trauma 77

Beautiful Healer 78

Soul Conversations 79

Easy to Love 80

Needs vs Wants 81

Pure Attraction 82

Speak Your Truth 83

breathe

purging

Insufficient Funds

we were never anchored.
our relationship
was simply transactional,
never reaching deep
into the core of our being…
I gave you what you needed
and never got what I needed.
I truly believed that my valuable deposits
would soon allow for endless withdrawals.
But every single transaction returned with insufficient funds.

Unfortunate Truth

it's funny that,
when you're unavailable,
your value is recognized
while your presence never was.

Self-Reflection

I feel like a child
begging you to love me…
Every time I hurt,
you seem to call it drama.
I'm tired of chasing someone
who doesn't want to be loved.
I'm no longer begging you to love me.
I know my worth.
Maybe it's about time
that you figure out yours.

Candid Truth

The love we had
was never love.
I learned that the instant
you left me
and loved someone else.

Self-Worth

Remember when
I gave you all I had
and you took it
and poured it into others?

Thank you for that.

Now I know that
I can't pour myself
into people
who are too small
to receive my gifts.

Damaged Goods

Let's be honest:
You knew
you did not need me,
you knew
you did not love me,
you knew
you could not give me

all that I needed.

I needed to be held.
I needed to be seen and heard.
I needed you to need me.

But somehow,
we were

together.

I guess I never truly knew that
I needed you
to break my heart
in all the right places
so that I could
love in all the right ways.

Drained

Loving you sucked
the life out of me.
My dreams,
my goals,
my aspirations,
my identity…
You took them all from me
and created a real-life nightmare.

Always running toward nothing and running away from the unknown.
My quickened breath scurried to catch up with my heart palpitations
and all that I lost in loving you.

When did I become so gullible?

Self-Reflection

Why do I choose
to love broken people?

Emotionally unavailable and looking for love
in all the wrong places.

It's attraction…

Broken

*Trigger Warning

We were exploring as children
in the bathroom
alone.
We kissed each other
innocently
like we'd seen in the movies,
except we kept our eyes open.

The rusty hinges on the door
signaled someone else's presence.
We quickly jumped back.

"What are you guys doing?
John, you stupid fuck... Get out!"
"You... you've been a bad girl.
I should tell on you"

"Please don't..."

"I won't
Come over here
and let me show you
how it's done.
We can practice together.
It will be our little secret."

A pit formed in my stomach.
The lights went out.
He was 16 and I was 5…

I felt broken.

Hide

I used to love
playing hide-and-seek.
But now,
it feels like I am hiding
to save my life
from a monster;
a predator.

Parasite

Trigger Warning

I still remember
how you sat me on your lap
in a crowded room
and had your way with me…

You were a parasite
Living off of me and seeking shelter in my body.
And I was your unwilling host.

Confused

Trigger Warning

If my dad was alive,
he would have murdered you
for even poking me,
but he's dead—
and Mom is mourning.

You threatened to kill
the only parent I have left.
I'm scared and confused.
I feel alone…

Memories

Trigger Warning

We were mourning,
but you were feeding
on your prey: me.
It was torture living in that house.

It became routine:
You'd give me the signal
With your eyes and a nod,
then I'd follow you
to an isolated room—
usually the bathroom.

It was there that I learned
everything I wanted to unlearn.
You'd turn on the water
to drown out any sound.
I still remember your scent:
your adolescent musk—
almost vile.

Vile like the acts committed in that room.
You forced yourself into my mouth
and watched the water flow out of the faucet.
I want to forget,
but water has memory.

Hide & Seek

*Trigger Warning

I spent what felt like an eternity
running from you—
It felt like an eternity.

We were finally leaving this hellhole.
Mom had decided to pick herself up
And live life.
Dad wasn't coming back;
She had to get back on her feet.

It was time to go,
so I packed up all of my stuff,
along with all the shattered pieces of me
on that bathroom floor and left,
feeling broken.

Awakening

Trigger Warning

He beat the fucking daylights out of her.
A simple conversation about
Bills, responsibility, and partnership
led to her being pummeled.

It was the first punch that did it:
Landed right over her right eye,
Revealing the eye socket.
His rings, the one with the bull,
had torn the skin around her eye.

She hit the ground.

The pounding of his foot on her
back
stomach
head—
Everywhere!

Each kick
Resonated like the frenzy
of an African drum,
building up to the climax.

Then, suddenly, silence…

She peeked through her bleeding eye
and saw the chair:
It was descending
slowly but purposely
to punctuate the end.

Silence invaded the space
as she welcomed darkness.

Involuntarily,
her lifeless hand crept up
to lessen the blow.
A flash appeared as her hand
met the chair.
She squinted, shocked at the fact that
her chest was still rising and falling—
and it was in the light.
Clear as day,
she saw her deceased mother
holding the chair with her.
"It's not your time," she uttered.

Amazed at the fact that the chair
was in her hand,
a sudden fear overcame him,
so he dropped the chair
and walked out of her life.

I wasn't there to see it,
but her scars—
bloody, swollen, disfigured
and bruised—
told the story.

Women are Warriors.
Royalty resides in our beings.
Mom, you are Royalty.
Thank you for reminding us!

If It Sounds Like You, It's You

Fuck you
and grow up!
Sticking your dick in
everything that walks
isn't manly at all.
Your lack of self-control is weak.
Your inability to commit shows
a lack of dedication to your vows.

Your functioning in the dark
and living a double life
displays an inability
to walk in your truth.
Is this the definition of "man"?

Fucking loser!
Men like you ruin Queens
in an attempt to King yourself
because you forgot where you came from.

Sad case…

Blurred Lines

You told *me*
that *you* loved *me.*
butthen, *you* told*her*
that you loved her too…

Classic.

Selfish

Why is it that things always have to go your way?
Am I allowed to voice my opinion?
Can I want something different than your plan?
You're so selfish—
Or maybe I don't see my own worth…

Forgiveness

Sometimes, we hurt others
because we think that
it is the only way to respond.
You can't offer
what you've never been given,
so I forgive you.

asking

Manifestation

Creation begins with thought.
I imagined you
before I met *you*.

In between all of the hurt,
you were born.
In the midst of all of the lies,
our loyalty grew.
Through nights of loneliness,
the idea of you held me.
In times of discontent,
you were manifested.

Necessary Lessons

If you hurt me,
thank you.
If you cheated on me,
thank you
If you underestimated my worth,
thank you.
If you took my love for granted,
thank you.
If you overlooked me,
thank you.
If you chose them over me,
thank you.

If…
If only you took the time to see me.
I saw you…
I saw *all* of you,
but I'm not sure I ever really knew you.

Complacent

We become complacent
with the lies we tell
so much that we fear
the truth
that will awaken us.

Omission
is the greatest lie.

Broken Spirit

Broken
is the spirit
that allows the body
to be
disconnected from the pulse
of the soul
in exchange for
what seems like love.

Victim To Victor

The cheating,

lies,

broken promises,

invisibility,

second-place trophy…

The lovers

who never seemed to resemble me.

The seemingly justified poor treatment.

These are all things that I learned from

the minute I stopped asking "why me?"

and began asking "what now?".

Truth

Sometimes,
it's easier to pretend
that you don't know
the truth.

The truth hurts…

Self-Destruction

I remember the day
when I realized
that my lover
had murdered my soul,
and I wondered
if I would remain
a willing accomplice
to this crime…

Guilty

The empty call logs are
questionable.
The cryptic late-night messages are
concerning.
The quick runs to the gym are
suspicious.
The discomfort with your phone in my hand is
evidence.

Intuition

You can pretend not to know,
but we always know…
It's called women's intuition.

Choices

Stop saying that
you're staying
"for the kids".
All they see is
the lie you are living.

Choices…

Hard Truth

Wake up!
Love doesn't live here
and you know it.
Stop fooling yourself!
Convenience isn't fulfilling;
it's just easily
accessible.

shifting

Tough Conversations

Fear:
afraid to tell the truth
because it was never
a habit.

Vulnerability

Being vulnerable
can be difficult.
Being
bare
naked
unguarded
leaves room for so much
hurt and judgement.

Soul Work

Telling the truth
requires courage
and the truth is,
most of us aren't brave enough
to show up in our own skin
and
speak the words that quiver on the edge of our lips.

Instead, we fear being judged
and deflect our own issues onto the other,
holding them responsible for things
that we have never taken the time to heal.

Self-work is the most important work we can do, before showing up in any
relationship with another.
Heal your Self, and your Soul will love you.

Self-Hypnosis

Who taught you to only see your flaws,
but not your potential?
Who ripped your heart out
and broke it into a million pieces?
Who told you that your beauty isn't mesmerizing?
Who said they loved you
and then committed to others instead?
Who taught you that you are not worthy?
I'm sure the guilty party is reading this now…

Preparation

Every interaction
is an opportunity for you
to create the interactions
that you wish to experience.

You will get back the same energy
that you put out to others.
Be kind. Be Loving. Be compassionate.
Especially when it is most difficult to do.

Normalize Self-Love

You pretend to enjoy life,
but I know it's all part of the show:
the façade for the audience.
The happy family posts and the smiles
contradict the reality.

It is a life filled with
lies, deceit, and abuse
that you've normalized
through silence and inaction.

So, although you now know
that I am the best person to love you,
you don't recognize real love
because it's "abnormal".

If only you could turn within…
I finally did,
and I found a worthy woman.
So, I went out to find someone
who saw the same.

The Rage We Carry

I learned a lot
from watching you:
I learned that rage
isn't always visible.
It is often silent and corrosive,
and it can eat up your insides.

Anger is unhealthy.
Handle it
before it handles you…

allowing

Expectations

Remember:
You will only be treated
the way you allow others
to treat you.

Self-worth…

In Love with Me

Teach others how to love you.
Lead by example.
Acknowledge your…
value,
worth,
beauty.
Love yourself
completely and unconditionally.
Love yourself
in the way that you'd want others
to love you.

Be and feel
unapologetically beautiful.

Ode to My Single Mother

I remember overhearing a therapist
respond to her client…

An emotionally battered at home mom asked:
"If I leave him,
where would I go?
What would I do?"

Her therapists responded:
"You do what every single
Black woman in America does…
Figure it out."

It was in that moment when I realized…
My mother is
Superwoman.

Acknowledging Mom

Mom.

Single mother.

Immigrant.

Breadwinner.

Cook.

Disciplinarian.

Minimum wage worker.

Fearless.

Badass.

Mom.

Own Your Shit

Waiting for SOMEONE TO BE DIFFERENT
FOR you TO BE happy IS ABSURD.
Identify your needs and feed your soul.

Happiness comes from within.

Clarity

Don't blame anyone for your unhappiness.
They are not responsible,
so get up and do something
or shut up and hide behind
your rose-tinted glasses.

Self-talk…

Choose Wisely

There are two types of lovers in the world:
(1) Those who love in the open
and (2) those who love in the dark.

Either one is a **choice**.

Who are you?

1 or 2

Energy

Spend more time
with those who model the spirit
you wish to exhibit in the future.
Energy is contagious.

Time

Time with yourself isn't selfish;

it is a **right**.

Sometimes, we spend so much time looking out

that we forget to look within.

surrendering

Beautiful Dilemma

I've spent the past few months
getting to know you
for the beautiful person that you are
and falling more and more
in love with that person.

I look forward to
your calls, our talks, our text sessions,
random thoughts and other things.
Unfortunately, we don't have anything more
than that because we live so far:
no shared experiences,

no closeness,

no physical relationship,

no familiarity.

Exposed

Arriving like the sun:
subtly peeking,
slowly revealing,
then boldly exposed.

Arrived…

Falling

PART 1

First texting at night,
then at night and morning.
Eventually,
it became a ritual:
texting throughout the day.
I know myself,
and this was a huge indicator
that I liked you a little more than
I was ready to admit.

Falling…

PART 2

And it happened…
It came on suddenly…
I didn't even see it coming…

You said something,
and my heart fluttered—
a feeling that I have come to notice
as my deep love for *you*.

Mental Orgasm

Enthralled by the brawn
behind the words—
words that flowed effortlessly
and fluid conversations lasting hours…
The best mind-sex I've ever had.

Surrendering in Love

I remember it so clearly:
We had been talking for hours,
and it was evening when our conversation began.
At some point, the sun was rising.
We were physically exhausted,
but mentally stimulated.

It was August 1ˢᵗ,
and as I watched the sun rise through my window.
You watched it from yours a thousand miles away.
It just felt right so…
I admitted my love for you;
I could no longer hide the emotions from you.

Then, without warrant, you whispered:
"I love you too."
Then all of the tension in my body left me,
and your love spilled all over my soul.

Easy To Love

Water seems to
flow with ease
through me.
Just like that,
you appeared,
filling every inch of me
and crashing into the walls
of my heart.

Long Distance Relationship Struggles

There are times when you make me feel so good
I just want to hug you and hold you… or more.
Then reality sets in that this is not something
that I'm able to do.
Then I get frustrated
and maybe I take it out on you,
even though I know that we're both in the same boat.

As much as I try to stay positive and push past it,
I keep coming back to the same conclusion:
I can't love you this hard from this far away.
As much as I've tried to suppress this feeling,
it just keeps being an issue for me.

Frustrated

Yesterday when I got your package,
All I wanted was to hug and kiss you,
thank you and have you see how happy I was.
I needed that closeness with you at that moment.
I just needed *you*.

Instead, all I could get was
a text message or quick call
and then wait
to talk later that night.

Little Things

When I fantasize about us,
I envision stupid shit
that other people take for granted:
us taking a drive together,
a walk,
snuggling on a couch,
making a late-night run to a store,
lying in bed and laughing at silliness.
(I know, it sounds crazy…)

Overthinking

I do things throughout my day
And wish you were here to do them with me.
The times when I don't hear from you,
I'm wondering what you're up to and with who.

Lovers Then Friends

It's not easy,
and me not wanting to talk to you
is simply because I need to get
some of this shit out of my system.

There are too many emotions.

I guess I'm just not built like you…
I can't go from being in love with you
to just being friends immediately.

Space

I need to be "away" from you,
so my strongest feelings for you
can possibly subside or whatever.
At this point, I don't even want to meet.
It would just be a temporary fix
to a long-term problem.
We have responsibilities
that will keep us apart
for the foreseeable future...

and that's fine.

We have to live our lives.

Blinded

"I would love for you to find someone
close to you who will love *you*
only as a **priority**
and not as an escape.
You deserve a love that's devoted to *you*."

You are that person.
Be patient,
and it will reveal itself to you.

Soul Resonance

I knew you were "The One".
But I was there way before you;
I knew that I wanted you
and I'd wait to find out
how it feels to be loved by you…

You're worth the wait.
I'd rather wait for
one kiss with an angel
than endless nights
with an accessible partner.

Thoughts become Things

You always spent so much time
thinking…
thinking about
how difficult it is for us to be together
instead of noticing how easy
it can be.

receiving

Invested

Experience the highs and lows. Believe that the momentum of our love will catapult us from the lowest low. Feel that our passion generates enough fire to warm our hearts on the coldest night from one thousand miles away. Let yourself go in loving me. Trust me. Show me the parts of you that you have never exposed.

Disrobe fully…

    Expose your imperfections…

Watch me love the very part of you that others questioned. Point to the parts that need healing. Let me take away your pain, one kiss at a time. Allow me the time to explore, discover, and know your pain. Let me be your healer. Don't be afraid. Take my hand and walk with me. Live in the moment. You are my beginning…

Walking Blindly in Love

Naked…

    Bare…

        Exposed…

Completely vulnerable in love.

Gambling my emotions fearlessly knowing the wager, although heavy and risky, it is a worthy one.

The prize:

    you…

        your heart…

Wanting it all, every inch of it. Let your guard down. I want all of you. I'll have you no other way, but as naked and as bare as I am. I have an overwhelming need for you to join me on this mysterious journey, trusting the unknown limits of true love and not questioning what is destined by the need to control and safeguard hearts and emotions.

HoldMyHand.

W

    A

        L

           K with me.

Unconditional Prayer

I prayed for someone like you

without knowing

it was *you*

that I was praying for…

The first time I kissed you,
pieces of my being shifted and fell into place.
The moment we sealed lips,
you seemed to lose your breath,
releasing life into me—
the very life that was sucked out of me.

You held your breath…
my breath.
How did you know
that I needed resuscitation?

You held your breath
to breathe life into me…

Soul Love

I've made love to you before
from a distance.
I felt your kiss move down
my spine.
I felt your breathing against
my lips.

Eventually,
I was breathing for you
and you for me.
Slowly,
I let you in to join my soul.

It seems to know you
from another life.
It seems to have found
its true purpose:
to love you.

Contrast

It's easy to know
genuine love
when love has never been
genuine to you.
Contrast can be eye-opening.

Post-Relationship Trauma

Can you be loyal?
Can I trust you with my heart?
Will you cheat on me?
Will you lie to me?
Can I trust what you say?
You probably think I am
insecure
when really, this is all just
post-relationship trauma.

Beautiful Healer

You're beautiful.
I knew this even before my eyes
had ever met any physical part of you.
Your words are like the rhythm & blues to my soul.
You awakened something in me—
Something that I never thought I had.
It's awake now.
Thank you.

Soul Conversations

I guess it's true what they say:
You always know from the very beginning.
I knew you'd be mine forever
the moment I read your words
written on a page:
"loving you completely"
"wanting to make you mine"
"embracing all of you"
They just spoke to my soul
like no other,
and my soul responded—
and that scared me
simply because I knew
You were the one…

Easy To Love

I still remember how easy it was
to speak to you for hours:
Our conversation
began as the sun set
and ended at dusk.
Never running out of things to say,
but always running out of time to say
the things we needed to say.

It has always been easy to love you.

Needs vs Wants

I wanted so many things,
but never truly gave thought to what I needed.

You were exactly what I needed.
I needed a listener,
a supporter,
and an available partner.
Thank you for surpassing my expectations.

Pure Attraction

Your smile is addictive.
Laughter, contagious.
I want nothing more than
to have these lips
infect mine.

Speak Your Truth

Silenced by my past,
secrets lurking in my dreams
and hovering in my present.
Feeling enslaved
by the hidden truth
weighing on me.
Pressing the air out of my lungs,
struggling for breath.

Speak truth.
And suddenly, when breathing with ease,
the truth shall set you free.
Breathe.

Printed in Great Britain
by Amazon

83946432R00054